S[   ]

THE

CHILDREN

A GHOST STORY

CORAX

DOMINIC SELWOOD

Published in Great Britain by
CORAX
London

Visit our author website and blog
www.dominicselwood.com

ISBN 978-0-9926332-3-3

Cover design and typesetting by Odyssey Books
Set in Baskerville 11/15

ABOUT THE AUTHOR

Dominic Selwood is the Amazon no. 1 bestselling author of the crypto-thriller, *The Sword of Moses*. He is also the author of *Knights of the Cloister*, a history of the medieval Knights Templar and Knights Hospitaller. He writes for the UK's *Daily Telegraph* newspaper, and has appeared as a historical expert on numerous TV and radio programmes. He also acts as a historical consultant for film and industry. He studied at university in Oxford, the Sorbonne, London, Poitiers, and Wales, and has taught and lectured on warfare, religion, heresy, and all the fun stuff. He is an elected Fellow of the Royal Historical Society and an English barrister. He lives in London with his wife and two children, and has never stopped writing and researching.

By the same author

Fiction

THE SWORD OF MOSES

Short Stories

THE VOIVOD (*A GHOST STORY*)

Non-Fiction

KNIGHTS OF THE CLOISTER

For more information, visit
www.dominicselwood.com

TO

DELIA, INIGO, ARMINEL

FOR THEIR CONSTANT INSPIRATION

AND ENTHUSIASM

Oxford, 1904

IT WAS THE final formal hall dinner of the Michaelmas term, and, by tradition, all fellows attended. I ordinarily greatly enjoyed the gathering, being the last opportunity to see colleagues before the Christmas vacation emptied the college.

I found myself sitting next to Drower, a young man of science with whom I had not previously had cause to converse. As the candles wore down, the discussion around the high table fell to our plans for the vacation, and I confided that I proposed to take a trip to Norfolk, where I was intending to spend some time with a gazetteer, cataloguing the registers of a number of the parish churches. On hearing this, Drower became insistent that I stay at home with him, at Luxborough Hall. He would be coming and going, he explained, as he had certain affairs to attend to in the locality, but he assured me there was no more convenient place from which to explore the ecclesiastical geography of the Norfolk countryside.

The arrangements were made, and three days later I crunched across the snowy great quadrangle and out into town towards the railway station. I had with me Hendrick's *Rotuli diocesis sancte et individue trinitatis norvici* detailing the pipe rolls of Norwich cathedral, and I was much looking forward to reacquainting myself with it on the long journey.

It was late in the evening by the time the station trap brought me to Luxborough Hall, which the moonlight revealed to be a large, three-storey elevation of grey stone with an attractive balustrade adorning the roof. All was set in several dozen acres of forested parkland.

Most of the household had already retired, but Drower had kindly arranged for some cold pie, meats, cheeses, and fortified wine to be laid out for me, and he ensured I was comfortably settled before he retired for the night.

I awoke early the following day, but to my dismay the snow had fallen so heavily during the night that there would be no likelihood of me setting out on my researches to the outlying villages.

Drower left immediately after breakfast to attend a pressing engagement. He confided that he might be away for several days, and, appreciating my situation, volunteered me free use of the library if the weather kept me housebound. And so, after breakfast, I had the fire in the library built up, before settling myself there to begin exploring the not inconsiderable number of books and papers.

Judging from the bookplates, Drower's father had been a keen traveller. He had a particular fondness, it seemed, for southern Europe, evidenced by the large collection of volumes on the geology, flora, and fauna of much of the Mediterranean coastline, as well as a number of lesser-known almanacs and local histories of the region.

As I was exploring the shelf housing materials on southern Italy, Sicily, and the more obscure islands of the vicinity, I noticed a quarto-sized oxblood leather notebook nestled among a series of archaeological titles. I pulled it out and opened it to find the pages tightly filled with an antique but elegant hand, which, judging from the dates and contents, was that of Drower's father.

I thumbed briefly through the notebook, which treated of a journey he had made to southern Sardinia, and, finding the content of curious interest, located an atlas of the region before settling down to read the notebook along with the maps for reference.

This is the extraordinary and terrible story he told.

— o O o —

Sir Titus Drower, my host's late father, had some time earlier found himself in Naples, a region he discovered to be most sympathetic to his interests in Greek and Etruscan antiquities. Finding he had some time remaining after he had finished in that great city, he took a boat to the island of Sardinia, where, he had been informed, the remoter western coast held singular archaeological remains.

His journey eventually brought him to Iglesias on the island's southwesterly tip. There he found numerous monuments to keep himself occupied, and so put up at a local inn in a village some miles to the south.

The place in which he was staying was rustic in the local manner, and lacked the comforts of the mainland, but it was ideal for his work, offering him relative quiet and a good base from which to conduct his researches.

He spent several days surveying the antiquities clustered around the foothills of the Marganai, and was delighted to find that habitation in the region went back as far as the Phoenicians and Carthaginians, who had left tombs, menhirs, and other noteworthy vestiges.

On his second evening, while making for the village after enjoying a hill view of the curious volcanic Sant'Antioco and San Pietro islands some way out to sea, he fell into conversation with the local priest, one Don Anselmo. He found the cleric to be agreeable company, and they soon discovered a shared interest in the area's past. For instance, Drower was delighted to learn from Don Anselmo that San Pietro island, the more distant of the two, had been known as *Hieracon Nesos* to the Greeks, and as *Accipitrum Insula*, or Sparrowhawk Island, to the Romans.

Neither man having family attachments in the village, they soon took to dining together of an evening at the inn, where they enjoyed agreeable discussions on matters of mutual interest, and ate well of the simple but sturdy dishes produced by the innkeeper.

Don Anselmo, it transpired, was a mine of information on the locality. Although originally hailing from the mainland, he had trained at the university and seminary in neighbouring Cagliari, and had made the study of the island his own.

The good priest had shown Drower around his church, which the latter had politely appreciated, although as a devotee of classical antiquities, a twelfth-century Mediterranean village church held little of genuine interest for him. Nevertheless, he nodded gamely enough as he was shown the dogtooth- and chevron-carved doorway, a soot-blackened statue of the Virgin said to have been brought from the great Norman abbey of Monreale in Sicily, and what appeared to him a rather lengthy list of the church's priests going back to A.D. 1176. Had the squat, round-apsed edifice been built on the site of a temple of Artemis or Athena, Drower might have been more engaged. But, as it was, he indulged his new friend, and noted little other than the draught which whistled through the dim, ancient building, and some recent activities in the southeast corner of the cemetery where the sexton was clearing a plot for fresh graves.

However, after half a week of exploring and convivial dining with Don Anselmo in the evenings, Drower noted over a space of two days that a change had come over his new friend. Instead of his usual pleasant disposition, the clergyman had begun to look drawn, as if lacking sleep or suffering from some manner of nervous attack.

On the following day, Don Anselmo did not turn up at the inn for dinner at the usual hour, so, being in no especial hurry to eat, Drower made for the priest's house to see what was delaying his friend.

He was ushered into the humble building by a fraught housekeeper, whose local dialect Drower had great difficulty in deciphering. But presently he understood that Don Anselmo was in his room, and not to be disturbed.

Concerned for his friend, Drower nevertheless made his way upstairs, and, as he raised the latch on the bedroom door, perceived a piteous wail from within.

"In God's name, no!" he heard Don Anselmo's anguished voice, before he swung wide the door to reveal the priest in his bed, staring wide-eyed at the entrance to his chamber. "*Egredere, egredere, vir sanguinum et vir Belial,*"[1] Don Anselmo continued, raving at his visitor.

"My dear chap," Drower ventured, paling at the clergyman's hostile outburst. He strode into the room, taking in the priest's dishevelled state and expression of terror. "Whatever can be the matter?"

But as he reached the bedside, he could see that Don Anselmo was in no state to say anything intelligible. His eyes were blazing and bloodshot, and his skin was damp with a sheen of sweat. "*Nam et si ambulavero in medio umbrae mortis, non timebo mala, quoniam tu mecum es,*"[2] the cleric murmured, before sinking deliriously back into his pillow, repeating the phrases "wretched children" and what sounded to Drower like "Charon's obol".

With no delay, Drower hurried downstairs and procured a bottle of reviving spirits and a glass, before taking them upstairs and putting the restorative liquid to the lips of his anguished friend, who gradually became aware of Drower's presence.

"You must put it back," the priest rasped, when his eyes finally alighted on Drower. "You have to do it. Or they will not cease."

---

1   Come out, come out, thou bloody man, and thou man of Belial (Samuel 16:7).

2   Yea, though I walk through the valley of the shadow of death, I will fear no evil: for thou art with me (Psalm 23:4).

Drower frowned, whereupon the clergyman grasped his hand in a clammy grip. "What I should never have taken," he whispered. "It was the passage money, don't you see?" He sank back into the bed, visibly weakened from the exertion.

Drower refilled the small glass with more of the strong botanical spirits, and placed it again into the priest's unsteady hand.

"In the sacristy," Don Anselmo resumed hurriedly after taking the liquor. "An iron-bound box." He reached out and grasped Drower's upper arm. "You must return it." He stared emptily into the space ahead of him. "*Non timebis a timore nocturne*,"[3] he prayed quietly.

Drower's face must have registered a degree of confusion, for the priest continued with more urgency. "Where the sexton has been digging, there is an area of freshly disturbed … ." He blanched noticeably, and his voice lowered, "… a vault." His gaze turned to Drower, as if struck with a fresh fear. "I implore you, do not examine the contents, or linger. Only, replace the box, and seal the chamber again with the stone and earth. Do not ask me more. For the sake of our friendship, I implore you to do this."

Drower waited for the priest to say more, but the

---

3   Thou shalt not fear the terrors of the night (the Divine Office of Compline).

invalid had relapsed into a stupor. Drower took a moment to gather his thoughts and make a decision, then strode for the door. As he cast a look back at his wretched friend, he could hear him repeating softly over and again, *"Sinite parvulos ad me venire."*[4]

A multitude of questions and doubts were assailing Drower, but he had resolved to do just as his agitated friend requested.

After securing the church's great iron key from the housekeeper, Drower made his way once more out into the night. Despite the mildness of the autumn, he nevertheless found himself raising his collar against the wind, which seemed to have blown up out to sea, and had started to whip up the dust.

Arriving at the ancient building, he slid the key into the worn lock, and swung open the heavy, gnarled wooden door. On stepping forward into the darkened nave, he was greeted by the scent of centuries of incense and a musty floral odour hanging heavily in the air. He had neglected to bring a lantern or taper, but remembered sufficient of the church's layout from his previous trip to try to find his way to the sacristy.

Although not usually of a nervous disposition, the febrile condition of his friend had set Drower's senses on edge, and more than once, as he made his way

---

4   Suffer the little children to come unto me (Mark 10:14, Luke 18:16).

across the age-smoothed flagstones, he thought he saw small black shapes moving about him amid the gloom.

As he reached the northeast of the building, he found the door to the sacristy open, and was relieved when a pale shaft of moonlight allowed him to locate a candle and a packet of phosphorous matches on its shelves. Striking a stiff match, the flame spread light about the small airless room, and he soon spied the box to which his friend had alluded. It was no bigger than a small portmanteau case, and stood on a somewhat battered old quadricircular cope chest. Drower approached it slowly, taking in its appearance in detail.

The box was fashioned of an age-blackened iron, with three hoops bound tightly around it, each terminating in a lock where the lid met the front of the body. The depredations of time had rusted away the locks and parts of the lid, but it was still a serviceable receptacle. Drower edged closer, and, extending his right hand, pushed the lid upwards in order to gain sight of what lay within.

The top swung freely, and, to his surprise, he perceived that the box was filled almost to the top with dirty discs. Extracting one, he removed his pocket handkerchief and began to rub away at the accumulated grime, revealing a thin, corroded bronze coin. He was no numismatist, but the crude bas-relief cross and faded Latin legend strongly suggested to him an origin in the high middle ages. He took another, and found it to be copper, of similar design, and the same period.

Seeing the ancient coinage put him in mind of the phrase Don Anselmo had been deliriously repeating, "Charon's obol". But it made little sense why his friend had been referring to the ancient payment traditionally placed in the mouth of the departed to present to Charon, the boatman, who ferried them across the river to the land of the dead. Unsure of the significance of any of it, he clasped the box close to his chest, took up the candle, and headed out of the sacristy and once more into the main body of the medieval church.

Making his way back down the empty nave to the west door, he found the light from the candle only served to dazzle him, rendering the farther recesses of the church even blacker than before. As his eyes scanned the ancient architecture, he again felt the uneasy sensation that there were black shapes moving in the gloom. He was relieved when he reached the building's entrance and could once more feel the air on his face. He breathed it deeply, as he locked and secured the door behind him.

The wind quickly extinguished his candle, but the moonlight was sufficient to guide him along the south side of the church and up to the easternmost part of the cemetery, where he espied the disturbed earth he had seen several days earlier.

Reaching the spot, he dropped to his knees and peered into the freshly dug trench. At first his eyes revealed little, but as they grew accustomed to the sepulchral gloom, he could make out an aperture at the bottom of the pit where a stone slab had been removed, disclosing a void beneath.

Tying a handkerchief around his face to shield against any escaping bad air, he lowered himself into the trench, then lifted the box down and placed it on the moist earth beside the opening.

He shivered in the wind, seized by an inexplicable sensation that he was being watched by malevolent eyes set at numerous points around the perimeter of the cemetery. He noted the sexton's spade in the pit with him, and moved it closer for reassurance.

His feeling of being observed with hostile intent spurred him into quicker action. He had no desire to look into the vault below, not because of the warning from his friend, but he sensed instinctively that there was something there which he might struggle to apprehend without losing his reason.

With a burst of resolve, he took up the box and thrust it into the hole, lowering it as far as his arms would permit. Then he let go, anticipating the sound of it hitting the bottom of the vault, but heard only the whisper of the wind among the gravestones.

Seizing the stone slab that had been set aside, he heaved it back into place, sealing the vault shut. Then he shovelled spade-fulls of the banked-up earth over the stone until it could no longer be seen. He continued for half an hour until drenched in sweat, partly through exertion, but largely owing to the horror of knowing he was not alone in the cemetery, a sentiment growing stronger upon him by the minute.

When the task was done, he took the spade and leant it up against the eastern apse of the church, before walking as briskly as he could away from the cemetery and back towards Don Anselmo's house to report his accomplishments.

However, when he reached the priest's front door, he found the house in a state of extreme confusion. Neighbours were conversing in great agitation with the housekeeper, and Drower soon came to understand that Don Anselmo had left the house some while earlier, and was nowhere to be found.

Given the lateness of the hour and the clergyman's delirious state, it was feared that he might not have known his mind when he stepped out into the night, so a party was quickly assembled, and the village was combed. But even after a diligent search of every house and outlying building, there was no sign of the priest.

Undeterred, Drower continued the search further afield, passing the church and making for the south of the village, holding to the island's coastline, where the beach afforded him a moonlit sandy road.

Now alone, and unsure what drew him on, he again felt the sensation of being watched, just as he had in the graveyard some hours earlier.

With rising concern for his friend, he vainly scanned the area for any sign of life, until eventually his eyes were drawn to the far distance, where he could just make out a lone figure striding along a low promontory that stretched some way out into the sea.

It was impossible to discern the identity of the figure at such a great distance. Nevertheless, he realized with a rising sense of horror that what he had at first thought to be a black cloak flapping about the figure's body in the gusts of wind whipping the rocks seemed, in fact, to be something quite other.

Drower felt a descending numbness as he began to apprehend that the black shapes were separate and distinct from the man he was now sure was Don Anselmo. As he looked more closely, he was certain that the undulating black forms seemed to emanate from the water, and to be encircling the priest.

Drower cried out again and again to his friend, but the clergyman was too distant. Running towards the spot as fast as he was able, Drower sensed his innards turning to ice as he espied what looked like dark, misty arms rising from the shapeless miasma. It was as if they were waving or beckoning to the priest, drawing him towards them, pulling him down into the cold black waters.

Drower did not let up from shouting, but the figure had now waded into the inky sea so far that it covered his legs to the waist. As Drower watched with horror, the black shapes drew the priest ever onwards, guiding him into the depths of the infinite waters, until eventually his head disappeared under the cresting waves.

Drower shouted until he could shout no more, but the wind took his words, and there was, in any event, no one to hear.

On finally reaching the promontory, he scanned the sea for any sign of the clergyman, but there was nothing to behold, merely the agitated beating of the angry waves against the rocks and the sand.

Distraught, Drower turned and made for the village. By the time he arrived, first light was breaking, and he could see the sexton heading into the graveyard to continue his solitary task clearing more spaces for the dead.

Drower stopped him, breathlessly, and wildly recounted the terrible events he had witnessed. As the words tumbled out, he began to wonder if he had not been imagining it, if it had not been some trick of the light. Perhaps the priest had merely lost his mind and resolved to take his own life.

But as he described the ghastly scene, the sexton's

expression fell from one of hardened indifference to a contortion of conflicting emotions. Noticing this alteration in his interlocutor, Drower ceased his tale. After a pained silence, the gravedigger's reserve passed, and he began to speak, haltingly at first, sharing with the visitor a burden he had evidently long carried.

The Monsignor from Cagliari and the oldest families of the village had tried in vain to warn Don Anselmo when first he arrived, the sexton related. But the eager priest had brushed their pleas aside, dismissing them as rural superstition.

When Drower enquired more deeply about the nature of their concerns, the gravedigger again became reticent, but after some cajoling volunteered that, over the years, there had been many priests entrusted with the care of the village's souls, yet they rarely enjoyed a quiet old age. At this, Drower recalled the lengthy board of incumbents he had seen at the ancient church, and shuddered involuntarily.

The misfortune was an ancient one, the sexton confided, his face growing ashen. In the days of the old popes, Christian knights wearing the sign of the cross had conquered the faraway lands of Christ, and ruled it as they did the nations this side of the sea. But then servants of the Devil had preached that children should also go. The call was met, and villages emptied of their youngest, even as far as the lands of the

Germans, where a man in pied clothing and piping a flute had charmed the innocent to follow him.

The sexton gazed towards the grave where Drower had been working not several hours earlier. Two vast boatloads of children had finally weighed anchor from Marseille. One ship had made straight for the slave markets of North Africa, where the fair cargo was sold by wicked merchants and never heard of again. The other had foundered in a storm, right there, the sexton indicated the islands just off the coast, against the outlying rocks of San Pietro.

The gravedigger paused and crossed himself in the manner traditional in those parts. It was the curse of the doomed children, he confessed, his voice low and fearful. For centuries they had taken their revenge on the priests of the area, and on the Church that sent them to their deaths.

Drower had heard enough, and left the sexton to his melancholy work, hurrying on back to the centre of the village as the morning light was breaking fully over the eastern mountains.

On approaching the largest cluster of houses, he became aware of a cry going up from the beach beyond them. As he hurried down to the scene of the commotion and joined the weary villagers gathering around, the tragedy revealed itself.

There, prostrate in a small boat, lay the lifeless, sodden body of Don Anselmo, wearing only his bed dress and a rough outer cloak. From the conversation that ensued, Drower understood that men bearing the cadaver had rowed over from the island of San Pietro, where the dead clergyman had been washed in with the morning tide.

What seemed to be causing the boatmen the most disquiet, however, was that Don Anselmo's pockets, and even his mouth, were crammed full of what appeared to be heavily water-damaged old coins.

— o O o —

Such was the terrible story I read in the notebook of Sir Titus Drower.

There were no further details in the rest of the volume, and, although I combed the library for any other papers which might have some bearing on the dreadful tale, I found nothing other than that the library's handsomely bound editions of Alberic of Trois-Fontaines, Matthew Paris, and Vincent of Beauvais were all unusually worn at the point of their narration detailing the ill-fated Children's Crusade of A.D. 1212.

I remained at Luxborough Hall, and, as the weather soon cleared, I was eventually able to conduct my intended researches into a good number of the local parish churches.

When Drower returned from his affairs, I drew his attention to his father's notebook detailing the trip to Sardinia, which my friend read with an increasing pallor.

When he finished, he commented only briefly, and visibly shaken, that despite numerous family travels which took them near to several coasts, his father had always entertained a morbid terror of the sea. He had fiercely forbidden any of the children so much as to approach the shallowest of waters, although on such journeys he himself stood on rocky outcrops for unfathomable hours, staring resolutely at the ever-changing waters through an old brass telescope, as if waiting for something.

Praise for

THE SWORD OF MOSES

Amazon no. 1 Bestseller

'One of the Top 5 religious thrillers of all time'
BESTTHRILLERS.COM

'Rollercoaster crypto-thriller …
move over Lara Croft!'
Five Stars, Editor's Pick of the Week
DAILY EXPRESS

'A fast-paced Biblical thriller backed by impeccable
research. Fans of The Da Vinci Code will love this!'
**J F PENN, USA TODAY BESTSELLING AUTHOR OF
THE ARKANE SERIES**

'Without doubt one of the best books of 2013'
DREAMING.COM

'Brilliant'
HAMPSHIRE CHRONICLE

'Epic'
CIPHERMYSTERIES.COM

Lightning Source UK Ltd.
Milton Keynes UK
UKHW051306280921
391258UK00015B/214